THE IONIAN CYCLE

THE IONIAN CYCLE

by William Tenn

Spaceship Survivors

The tiny lifeboat seemed to hang suspended from its one working rear jet, then it side-slipped and began to spin violently downwards to the sickly orange ground of the planet.

Inside the narrow cabin, Dr. Helena Naxos was hurled away from the patient she was tending and slammed into a solid bulkhead. The shock jolted the breath out of her. She shook her head and grabbed frantically at an overhead support as the cabin tilted again. Jake Donelli glared up from the view-screen where the alien earth expanded at him and yelled across the control table:

"Great gravities, Blaine, soft jet! Soft jet before we're pulped!"

The tall, balding archaeologist of what had once been the First Deneb Expedition waved tremulous hands at the switches before him.

"Which—which button do you press?" he quavered. "I f-forget how y-you soften those forward things."

"You don't press any—oh, wait a minute."

The spaceman tore the restraining straps away and bounded out of his seat. He seized the projecting edges of the table and made his way strainingly around it as the lifeboat spun faster in great swoops.

Dr. Archibald Blaine was squeezed against the back of his chair when Donelli reached him.

"I forgot the button," he mumbled.

"No button, doc. I told you. You jerk this toggle—like so. You haul this switch over—like so. Then you turn the little red wheel around twice. Does it. Whew! Now things are smoother!"

Donelli let go of the table as the forward softening jets caught on and straightened the vessel into a flat glide. He walked back to the main control bank, followed by Blaine and the woman biologist.

"The sea?" Helena Naxos asked at last, lifting her eyes from the view-screen. "That *is* the sea?"

"Nothing else but," Donelli told her. "We used up all but about a cupful of fuel trying to avoid falling into this system's sun—if you can call two planets a system! We're operating the cupful on the one main jet left unfused when the *Ionian Pinafore* blew up. Now we've overshot the continent and riding above the sea without a paddle. Good, huh? What'd he say the sea was made of?"

Dr. Douglas Ibn Yussuf propped himself on his uninjured elbow and called from his bunk:

"According to the spectroscopic tabulations you brought me an hour ago, the seas of this planet are almost pure hydrofluoric acid. There is a good deal of free fluorine in the atmosphere, although most of it is in the form of hydrofluoric acid vapor and similar combinations."

"Suppose you save some of that good news," Donelli suggested. "I know all about hydrofluoric acid being able to eat through almost anything and its grandmother. Tell me this: how long will the Grojen shielding on the hull stand up under it? An estimate, Doc."

*

With puckered brow, the Egyptian scientist considered. "If not replaced, say anywhere—oh, anywhere from five terrestrial days to a week. Not more."

"Fine!" the pale spaceman said happily. "We'll all be dead long before that." His eyes watched the view-screen.

"Not if we find fuel for the converter and tanks," Blaine reminded him sternly. "And we know there's contra-Uranium on this world—a little, at any rate. The spectroscope showed it. That's why we headed here after the disaster."

"So we know there's fuel here—good old compact Q. Okay, if we landed on one of the continents maybe we'd have scratched a miracle on the chest and found some Q before the converter conked out. Then we could have repaired the other jets and tried to get back to a traffic lane, powered up the transmitter and radioed for help, done all sorts of nice things. But now that we're going to do our fall on the first island I see, what chance do you think we have?"

Blaine looked angrily at his two colleagues and then back at the small, squat spaceman with whom destiny and a defective storage tank aboard the *Ionian Pinafore* had thrown them.

"But that's ridiculous!" he said. "Landing on an island will reduce our chances of finding contra-Uranium from an improbability to an impossibility!

It's rare enough in the universe, and after we've been fortunate enough to find a planet containing it, Jake, I demand—"

"You demand nothing, Doc," Donelli told him, shoving belligerently up against his lean academic frame. "You demand nothing. Back on the expedition ship maybe the three of you were big-time operators with your degrees and all, and I was just Jake—broken from A.B. to Ordinary Spaceman for drunkenness when we lifted from Io. But here, I'm the only man-jack with a lifeboat certificate and the laws of space put me in supreme command. Watch your language, doc: I don't like to be called Jake by the likes of you. You call me Donelli from here on in, and every once in a while, you call me Mr. Donelli."

There was a pause in the cabin while the archaeologist's cheeks puffed out and his frustrated eyes tried to pluck a reply from the overhead.

"Mr. Donelli," Helena Naxos called suddenly. "Would that be your island?" She gestured to the view-screen where an infinitesimal blot upon the sea was growing. She smoothed her black hair nervously.

Donelli stared hard. "Yeah. It'll do. Suppose you handle the forward jets—uh, Dr. Naxos. You saw me explaining them to Blaine. I wouldn't trust that guy with a falling baseball on Jupiter. 'I forgot which button,'" he mimicked.

She took her place on the opposite side of the control table as Blaine, with tightened facial muscles, went over to Ibn Yussuf's bunk and whispered angrily to the injured man.

"You see," Donelli explained as he moved a lever a microscopic distance. "I don't want to hit an island any more than you folks do, Dr. Naxos. But we can't afford to use up any more fuel crossing an ocean as big as this. We may be able to make another continent, yes, but we'll have about fifteen minutes of breathing time left. This way, the converter should run for another two, three days giving us a chance to look around and maybe get some help from the natives."

"If there are any." She watched a dial needle throb hesitantly to a red mark. "We saw no cities on the telescanner. Although, as a biologist, I confess I'd like to investigate a creature with a fluorine respiration. By the way, Mr. Donelli, if you will allow me to call you Jake, you may call me Helena."

"Fair enough—hey, you watching that dial? Start softening jets. That's right. Now over to half. Hold it. Hold it! Here we go! Grab something everybody! Dr. Yussuf—lie flat—flat!"

He flipped the lever over all the way, slammed a switch shut and reached frantically for the two hand grips on the control table.

An emery wheel seemed to reach up and scrape the bottom of the hull. The emery wheel scraped harder and the whole ship groaned. The scrape spread along the entire bottom half of the lifeboat, rose to an unbearably high scream in sympathy to which every molecule in their bodies trembled. Then it stopped and a vicious force snapped their bodies sideways.

*

Donelli unstrapped himself. "I've seen chief mates who did worse on the soft jets—Helena," was the comment. "So here we are on good old—What's the name of this planet, anyway?"

"Nothing, so far as I know." She hurried over to Dr. Ibn Yussuf who lay groaning in the cast which protected the ribs and arm broken in the first explosion of the *Ionian Pinafore*. "When we passed the system on our way to Deneb a week ago, Captain Hauberk named the sun Maximilian—after the assistant secretary-general of the Terran Council? That would make this planet nothing more than Maximilian II, a small satellite of a very small star."

"What a deal," Donelli grumbled. "The last time I had to haul air out of a wreck, I found myself in the middle of the Antares-Solarian War. Now I get crazy in the head and ship out on an expedition to a part of space where humanity's just thinking of moving in. I pick a captain who's so busy buttering up to scientists and government officials that he doesn't bother to check storage tanks, let alone lifeboats. I haul air with three people—no offense, Helena—who can't tell a blast from the Hole in Cygnus and they get so cluttered up trying to seal the air-locks that, when the secondary explosion pops off from the ship, it catches us within range and blooies most of our jets and most of our Q. Then, to top it off, I have to set down on a planet that isn't even on the maps and start looking for the quart or two of J that may be on the surface."

She eased the scientist's cast to a more comfortable position and chuckled.

"Sad, isn't it? But ours was the only boat that got away at that. We were lucky."

Donelli began climbing into a space suit. "We weren't lucky," he disagreed. "We just happened to have a good spaceman aboard. Me. I'll scout around our island and see if I can find any characters to talk to. Our only hope is to get help from the folks here, if any. Sit tight till I get back and don't touch any equipment you don't understand."

"Want me to come with you—er, Donelli?" Dr. Blaine moved to the space suit tack. "If you meet anything dangerous—"

"I'll make out better alone. I've got a supersonic in this suit. And Doc—you might forget which button. Great gravities!"

Shaking his helmeted head, Donelli started the air-lock machinery.

The orange ground was brittle underfoot, he found, and flaked off as he walked. Despite the yellow atmosphere, he could see the complete outline of the island from the hill near the ship. It was a small enough patch of ground pointing reluctantly out of an irritated sea of hydrofluoric acid.

Most of it was bare, little dots of black moss breaking the heaving monotony of orange. Between the ship and the sea was a grove of larger vegetation: great purple flowers on vivid scarlet stems that held them a trembling thirty feet in the stagnant air.

Interesting, but not as interesting as fuel.

He had noticed a small cave yawning in the side of the hill when he climbed it. Sliding down, now, he observed its lower lip was a good bit from the ground. He started to enter, checked himself abruptly.

There was something moving inside.

With his metal-sheathed finger, he clicked on the searchlight imbedded in his helmet and with the other hand, he tugged the supersonic pistol from its clamps in the side of his suit and waited for its automatic adjustment to the atmosphere of the planet. At last it throbbed slightly and he knew it was in working condition.

They needed favors from the inhabitants and he didn't intend to do any careless dying, either.

Just inside the cave entrance the beam of his light showed a score of tiny maggot-like creatures crawling and feeding upon two thin blankets of flesh. Whatever the animals they were eating had been, they were no longer recognizable.

Donelli stared at the small white worms. "If you're intelligent, I might as well give up. I have an idea we can't be friends. Or am I prejudiced?"

Since they ignored both him and his question, he moved on into the cave. A clacking sound in his headphones brought him to a halt again, squeezing a bubbling elation back into his heart.

Could it be? So early and so easy? He drew the screen away from the built-in Geiger on his chest. The clacking grew louder. He turned slowly until the flashlight on his head revealed a half dozen microscopic crystals floating a few inches from one wall.

Contra-Uranium! The most compact, super-fuel discovered by a galactic-exploring humanity, a fuel that required no refining since, by its very nature, it could occur only in the pure state. It was a fuel for whose powerful uses every engine and atomic converter on every spaceship built in the past sixty years had been designed.

But six crystals weren't very much. The lifeboat might barely manage a take-off on that much Q, later to fall into the hydrofluoric sea.

"Still," Donelli soliloquized, "it's right heartening to find some so near the surface. I'll get an inerted lead container from the ship and scoop it up. But maybe those crystals have a family further back."

The crystals didn't, but someone or something else did.

Four large, chest-high balls of green, veined thickly with black and pink lines, throbbed upon the ground at the rear of the cave. Eggs? If not eggs, what were they?

WILLIAM TENN

Weird Beings

Donelli skirted them warily, even though he saw no opening in any of them. They were anchored to the ground, but they were unlike any plants he had seen in nine years of planet-jumping. They looked harmless, but—

"Well, grow me tentacles and call me a Sagittarian!"

The back of the cave divided into two tunnels which were higher and wider than their parent hollow. Smooth all around, Donelli might have taken them for the burrows of an immense worm, had he not noticed the regularly-spaced wood-like beams crossed upon each other at intervals in both shafts. The tunnels extended a good distance ahead, then curved sharply down and away from each other.

This was mining, this was engineering! Primitive, but effective!

Donelli hated to use up power in his helmet-transmitter, but he might run into trouble and it was essential that the three scientists learn of even the small amount of Q in the cave. After all, the creatures who built these tunnels might not know enough chemistry to appreciate his inedibility before they sampled him.

He turned on his headset. "Donelli to ship! Good news: I've found enough Q to keep us breathing until *after* this atmosphere burns through our Grojen shielding. We'll be able to sit around in our space suits for at least three days after the ship is eaten out from under us. Nice? You'll see the crystals about halfway into the cave. And don't forget to use an inerted lead container when you pick them up."

"Where are you going, Jake?" He recognized Helena's voice.

"Couple of tunnels at the rear of the cave here have regulation cross-supports. That's why we didn't see any cities when we came down. The smart babies on this world live underground. I'm going to try to talk them into a reciprocal trade treaty—if we have anything they want to reciprocate with."

"Wait a minute, Donelli," Blaine shouted breathlessly. "If you meet any intelligent aliens, it's more than possible they won't understand Universal Gesture-Diagram. This is an unexplored fluorine-breathing world. I'm an experienced archaeologist and I'll be able to communicate with them. Let me

11

join you."

Donelli hesitated. Blaine was smart, but he sometimes fumbled.

Helena came back on. "I'd suggest you take him up on it," her steady voice said. "Archibald Blaine may get switches confused with buttons, but he's one of the few men in the galaxy who knows all nine of Ogilvie's Basic Language-Patterns. If these miners of yours don't respond to an Ogilvie Pattern—well, they just don't belong in our universe!"

As Donelli still hesitated, she developed her point. "Look Jake, you're our commander and we accept your orders because you know how to cuddle a control board and we don't. But a good commander should use his personnel correctly and, when it comes to dealing with unknown extra-terrestials, Blaine and I have training that you've been too busy to acquire. You're a spaceman; we're scientists. We'll help you get your Q, then we'll take orders from you on how to use it."

A pause. "All right, Blaine. I'll be moving up the right-hand tunnel. And Helena—see that his space suit is all buttoned up before he leaves the ship? He can catch an awful cold in that yellow air."

The squat, pale spacehand took a firm grip on his sound pistol and walked delicately into the shaft. The ground here was of a firmer consistency than that on the surface: it supported his weight without either chipping or sagging. That was good. Nothing could come at him through the walls without his detecting it first.

He ducked under a cross-beam, his light momentarily pointing down. When he straightened again, he saw he had company.

At the far end of the tunnel, where it slanted down, several long, segmented beings were moving slowly toward him. There was only the faintest rustle in his headphones as they approached.

Donelli noticed with relief that only one of them had a weapon, a crude hand-ax without a handle. Come to think of it, though, an ax-head thrust forcefully might penetrate not his suit but—what was more dangerous—the Grojen shielding, leaving the metal exposed to the corrosive atmosphere. Not so good. But they didn't seem hostile.

WILLIAM TENN

*

As they arrived within a few feet of him, their speed decreased almost to immobility but their three pairs of three-clawed limbs pushed them to his side. Then they stopped, and the long thin hairy appendage on their heads brushed against his suit inquiringly and without fear. Their toothless mouths opened and made low gobbling sounds to each other.

They evidently had a language. Donelli saw the flat membrane on their backs that was obviously an ear, but he looked in vain for eyes. Of course, living underground in darkness, they were blind. A fat lot of help Universal Gesture-Diagram would be, even if they could understand it.

Something about the sectioned length of the bodies stretching behind them, something about their rich ivory color, was familiar. Donelli's mind tugged at his memory.

A terrific crash sounded in his ear phones. The three burrowers stiffened around him. Donelli turned and swore.

Blaine had entered the tunnel and smashed into one of the cross-beams. He was stepping over the fallen log now. His space suit seemed undented, but his self-confidence had not fared so well. Also a little bubble of earth formed over the area which had rested on the beam end.

The natives had rubbed their head filament upon the ground as if examining its intentions. Now, before Donelli could get started, they scampered down the tunnel toward the fallen support. Working in perfect coordination, without any apparent orders, they quickly lifted and inserted it in its former position. Then they began brushing against Blaine.

"Deep space, Doc," Donelli moaned as he came up.

"Sh-h-h—quiet!" The archaeologist had bent over the nearest burrower and was clicking his metal-enclosed fingers in an odd rhythm over its ear patch. The animal curved away for a moment, then began a low, hesitant gobbling to the same rhythm as the finger-clicks.

"Can—can you talk to it?" Donelli found it difficult to see the old man as anything but a doddering ineffectual.

13

"Ogilvie Pattern Five. Knew it. *Knew* it! Those three-clawed feet and the sharp curve of the ax. Like to investigate the material of the ax—noticed the pointed tip right off. Had to be an Ogilvie Five language. Can I talk to it? Of course! Just need a minute or two to establish the facets of the pattern."

The spaceman's respect for the academic life grew rapidly as he saw the other two aliens edge under the metallic hand and commence gobbling in turn.

They were joining the conversation, or the attempt at one.

Blaine began to stroke the side of one of the creatures with his other hand. The gobbling acquired a note of surprise, became staccato.

"Amazing!" Blaine said after a while. "They mine everything, and completely refuse to discuss the existence of surface phenomena. Most unusual, even for an Ogilvie Five. Do you know where they get their supporting beams? From the roots of plants. At least, that's what they seem to be from their description. But—and this is what the Galactic Archaeological Society will consider significant—they cannot seem to grasp the concept of plant blossoms. They know only of the roots and the base of the stem. Their social life, now, is strangely obscure for so elementary a culture. But perhaps it might better be termed simple? Consider the facts—"

"You consider them," Donelli invited. "I'm thinking of the Q we need. All this space suit power drain is cutting so many hours off our total breathing time. Find out what they'd consider a good trade and ask them to move up into the cave ahead so that I can show them what contra-Uranium looks like. We'll supply them with inerted lead containers for picking up the stuff. How far do their tunnels run?"

"All around the planet, I gather. Under the sea and under the continents in a crossing, branching network. I don't anticipate any difficulty. Being the dominant intelligent life-form of the planet, and not particularly carnivorous, they're really quite friendly."

*

Blaine's fingers clicked questioningly at the nearest alien and he stroked its side with short and long rolls of his hand. The creature seemed confused and gobbled to its companions. Then it moved back. Blaine clicked and stroked once more.

"What's the matter, doc? They look angry now."

"My suggestion of the cave. It's evidently under the strongest of taboos. These are barbarians, you understand, just emerging into a religious culture-matrix, and a powerful taboo takes precedence over instinct. Then, too, living in the tunnels, they are probably agoraphobic—"

"Look out! They're trying to pull some fancy stuff!"

One of the aliens had scuttled under Blaine's feet. The archaeologist tottered, crashed to the ground. The other two burrowers grasped his long arms between their claws. Blaine struggled and rolled desperately, looking like a confused elephant attacked by jackals.

"Donelli," he gasped, "I can't talk to them while they're holding my arms. They're—they're carrying me!"

The pair of burrowers were dragging the old man's body down the tunnel with gentle but insistent tugs. "Don't worry, doc. They won't get by me. That must have been one powerful taboo you broke when you mentioned the cave."

As Donelli advanced to meet the group, the alien who had upset the archaeologist scurried ahead to confront him. A forward claw held the small ax-head well back for a thrust.

"Look, fella," Donelli said placatingly. "We don't want any trouble with you, but we aren't carrying too much power right now and the doc's suit would run down in no time if you took him any deeper. Now why don't you act business-like and let us show you what we need?"

He knew his words carried no meaning in themselves, but he had had enough experience of unusual organisms to know that a gentle attitude frequently carried the conviction of its gentleness.

Not here, though. The claw snapped forward suddenly and the ax-head spun toward his visored face with unexpected velocity. Donelli jerked his head to one side and felt the pointed tip of the weapon scratch the side of his helmet. The slight buzzing in his right ear was replaced by an empty roaring:

that meant the ear phone had gone dead, which in turn meant the Grojen shielding had been chipped off leaving the hydrofluoric vapors free to eat through the metal.

"This is no good. I guess I'll have to—" The burrower had retrieved the ax in a lightning scamper and had it poised for another throw. As Donelli brought his supersonic up, he marveled at the creature's excellent aim despite its lack of vision. That long, hairy filament waving from the top of its head evidently served to locate his movements better than the finest radarplex on the latest space ships.

Just before he blasted, he managed to slip the intensity rod on the top of the tube down to non-lethal pitch. The directional beam of high-frequency sound tore down at the burrower and caught it with the claw coming around again. It stopped in mid-throw, stumbled backwards, and finally collapsed into unconsciousness upon the orange ground. The ax-head rolled out of its opened claw.

Blaine protested with a grunt as he was dropped by the other two. They ran up to the fallen burrower and edged around his body insistently. Donelli held his supersonic ready for further developments.

What happened took him completely by surprise.

*

In a series of movements so rapid that he could hardly follow it visually, one of the aliens snatched up the ax-head while the other lifted the creature Donelli had blasted to its back. They rolled up the slope of the tunnel and scurried past him on either side, the fluorine atmosphere almost crackling with their passage. By the time the spaceman had whirled, they were gone down the far end of the shaft where it dipped into the interior of the planet.

"They sure can hurry when they feel they have to," Donelli commented as he helped the older man to his feet. "Which is what I have to do if I want to get back to the ship before I start sneezing hydrofluoric acid."

While they sped as rapidly as the heavy suits would permit up the tunnel and through the cave, Blaine wheezed an explanation: "They were quite friendly until I mentioned the cave. There seems to be so much sacredness connected with it in their minds that my mere invitation to go there reduced me from an object of great interest to one of the most abysmal disgust. They were indifferent to any wants of ours in reference to the place. Any suggestion of taking them along is enough to precipitate a violent attack."

Donelli wondered if he were imagining the smarting sensation in his eyes. Had fluorine started to seep in already? Fortunately, they were at the mouth of the cave.

"Not so nice," he said. "The Q around here isn't enough to make our ship give out with a healthy cough, and we'll need their help to get any more. But we can't tell them what we want unless they go to the cave with us. Besides, after this fracas, they may be a trifle hard to meet. Why were they carrying you away?"

"To sacrifice me to some primitive deity as a placative measure, possibly. Remember they are in the early stages of barbarism. The only reason we weren't attacked immediately is because they are easily the dominant life-form of this world and are confident of their ability to cope with strange creatures. Then again, they might have wanted to investigate me—to dissect me—to examine my potentialities as food."

They rang the air-lock signal and clambered in.

Race Against Time

Hastily Donelli stripped off his space suit. There was a thin scar on the metal of the helmet where the Grojen shielding had been scratched away and HF vapor eaten in. A little longer out there and he would have been doomed!

"Hullo!" For the first time, he noticed that almost one-third of the cabin was taken up by a great transparent cage, one corner of which was occupied by a relaxed red creature with folded black wings. "When did the vampire kid arrive?"

"Ten minutes ago," Helena Naxos replied. She was adjusting a temperature-pressure gauge at the side of the cage. "And he—she—it didn't arrive: I carried it inside. After Dr. Blaine left, I went over the island with the telescanner and noticed this thing flying in from the sea. It went right to those purple flowers and began cutting off sections of the petals and putting them in a sort of glider made out of vines and branches that it was towing. The things obviously cultivate vegetation. That patch out there is one of their gardens."

"Imagine!" the archaeologist breathed. "Another civilization in embryo—avian this time. An avian culture would hardly build cities. But this is a culture where the glider comes before the wheel."

"So you put on a space suit and went out to get it." Donelli shook his head. "You shouldn't have done that, Helena. That creature might have packed a wallop."

"Yes, I considered the possibility. But I didn't know if you two were going to hit anything important, and this winged thing looked as if it might prove to be a link between us and this world. Its ability to fly, in particular, while we are grounded could prove valuable. It was fairly quiet when I approached, neither scared nor angry, so I tried the little Ogilvie I know—pattern one. Didn't work."

"Of course not," Dr. Blaine told her positively. "This is obviously Ogilvie Language-Pattern Three. Consider the hinged wings, the primitive glider you mentioned, the husbandry of flowers. It has to be an Ogilvie Three."

"Well, I didn't know that, Dr. Blaine. And it wouldn't have helped me much if I had. Ogilvie is a little too rich for a poor female biologist's blood. At any rate, after communication broke down—or never got started—this thing ignored me and prepared to fly away with its loaded glider. I squeezed some supersonic at it—low-power of course, brought it down and came in to ask Dr. Ibn Yussuf's advice on how to build a compartment that would permit us to keep it in the ship without killing it by oxygen poisoning."

"Must have used up an awful lot of Q, Helena! I notice you have pretty elaborate temperature and pressure controls as well as HF humidifiers and in-grav studs. And that loud-speaker system is wasteful."

Dr. Ibn Yussuf groaned up in his bunk and called across the cabin. "It does reduce our supply of contra-Uranium to the danger point, Donelli, but, under the circumstances, we thought we were justified. Our only hope is to get aid from the inhabitants of this planet, and we can't get aid unless we can hold them long enough to explain our position and wants to them."

"You have something there," Donelli admitted. "I should have made a stab at bringing back one of those specimens we ran into, not that it would have done much good from the way they acted. Hope you have more luck with this avian character. Treat him—her—it lovingly for he—she—it's our last chance."

Then he and Blaine told her about the burrowers.

"I wish I had been with you," she exclaimed. "Think of it: two barbaric civilizations—one on the surface and the other in the tunnels—developing in complete unconsciousness of each other on the same planet! The burrowers know nothing of the avians, do they Dr. Blaine?"

"Absolutely nothing. They even refuse to discuss the matter. Surface life is a completely alien concept to them. Their agoraphobia—fear of open places—probably has much to do with their reluctance to accompany us to the cave or even the tunnel entrance. Agoraphobia—Hm-m-m. Then these winged creatures might well be claustrophobic! That would be a catastrophe! We'll find out in a moment. It's opening its eyes. Where is that loud-speaker arrangement?"

Helena moved competently to the microphone and tucked a lever past several calibrations. "You may know its Ogilvie Pattern, doctor, but it takes a biologist to give the sound frequency at which it can hear best!"

*

As Blaine began experimental dronings and buzzings into the instrument, the creature inside the transparent cage opened its wings in a series of hinged movements and revealed the whole rich redness of its small body. It crawled under the loud-speaker and spread open a mouth that was slit up and down instead of sideways. The black wings beat slowly as it gained interest, reflecting cheerful yellow streaks in their furrows. The two tentacles under its jaw lost their stiffness and undulated in mounting excitement.

This would take some time. Donelli walked to the telescanner and faced Dr. Douglas Ibn Yussuf.

"Suppose we get this fellow to cooperate. Where's a good place to tell it to look for Q?"

The chemist lay back and considered. "You are familiar with Quentin's theory of our galaxy's origin? That once there were two immense stars which collided—one terrene, the other contra-terrene? That the force of their explosion ripped the essence of space itself and filled it with ricocheting terrene and contra-terrene particles whose recurring violence warped matter out of space to form a galaxy? According to Quentin, the resulting galaxy was composed of terrene stars who are touched every once in a while by contra-terrene particles and go nova. The only exception is contra-Uranium, the opposite number of the last element in the *normal* periodic table, which will not explode as long as it is isolated from the heavy elements near its opposite number on the table. Thus in a fluorine atmosphere, with a bromide soil and—"

"Look, Doc," Donelli said wearily. "I learned all that in School years ago. Next you'll be telling me that it's thousands of times more powerful than ordinary atomic fuels because of its explosive contra-terrene nature. Why is it that you scientists have to discuss the history of the universe before you give a guy an answer to a simple question even in a crisis like this?"

"Sorry, son. It's difficult to break the habits of an academic lifetime, even in times of a deadly emergency. That's your advantage: you're accustomed to operate against time, while we like to explore a problem thoroughly before attempting a mere hypothesis. Science is a caution-engendering discipline, you see, and—

"All right. I won't digress into a discussion of the scientific attitude. Where would you find contra-Uranium on a planet that's been shown to possess it? Near the surface, I'd say, where the lighter elements abound. You've already found some in a cave on this island? That would indicate that it was forced explosively to the surface, the only place it could exist, when the planet was in a formative state. If there is other contra-Uranium on this world, there must be other caves like the one here."

Donelli waved him to silence and bent over the telescanner. "Good enough. Deep space and suppressed novas, Doc. That was *all* I wanted to know! Now I'll see how much I can find out before I use up the dregs of our power."

He swept the beam across the sickly sea and up the coast-line of the continent until he saw a dark spot in the orange ground. Then, nudging the telebeam into the cave, he saw at last the few shimmering crystals that meant precious Q. He tried other apertures here and there, convincing himself that, while there was little enough in any one cave, the planet as a whole possessed more than they required. The sight of all the unobtainable Q on the telescanner screen made Donelli sweat with exasperation.

He made another discovery. Leading down, in the rear of every cave was at least one tunnel that denoted the presence of the burrowers.

"If only we could have made them understand," Donelli murmured. "All of our problems now would have been orbital ones."

He rose and turned to see how his shipmates were doing with the winged alien. "Great gravities, what did you *do* to it?"

The avian was back in a corner of the fluorine-filled compartment, its hinged black wings completely screening its body from sight. The wings pressed down harshly as if the creature were attempting to shroud itself out of its environment.

*

Dr. Archibald Blaine, his hands cupped over the microphone, was *chuk-chuking* urgently, droning repetitiously, humming desperately. No apparent effect. The black wings squeezed tighter into the corner. A fearful, muffled gulping came over the loud-speaker in the wall.

"It was the mention of the cave, again," Helena Naxos explained, her pleasant face betraying worry. "We were doing fine, going from 'howd'yedo's' to 'how'veyebeen's'—the girlie was beginning to tell us all about her complicated love-life—when Dr. Blaine asked if she had ever been inside the cave. Period. She crawled away and started to make like the cover of a hole."

"They can't do this to us!" Donelli yelled. "This planet is practically crawling with Q which we can't get because we don't have the Q to cross a hydrofluoric acid sea. The only way we can get it is for these babies to haul it over, either underground through tunnels or across the sea. And every time Blaine starts talking about the caves where the Q is lying around, they go neurotic on him. What's the *matter* with the caves? Why don't they like them? *I* like the caves!"

"Take it easy, Jake," Helena soothed. "We're up against a basic taboo in two separated cultures. There must be a reason for it. Find the reason and the problem is solved."

"I know. But if we don't find it soon we'll be nothing but fancy fluorine compounds."

The woman returned to Dr. Blaine. "Is it possible you could reawaken her interest by offering some gift? A superior glider, for example, or power-driven flight."

"I'm working on it," he replied testily, withdrawing his mouth from the microphone. "To creatures on the threshold of civilization, however, superstition takes precedence over mechanical innovations. If it's *only* superstition—that's another thing we don't know. Could it be the contra-Uranium crystals they're afraid of?"

Dr. Ibn Yussuf raised himself on his sound arm. "That is doubtful. Their chemical composition contains no elements heavier than barium, according to the spectroscope. Thus no contra-atomic chain reaction would be set off by their bodies coming in contact with the crystals. Perhaps the mere existence of the crystals upsets them."

Blaine frowned. "No. Unlikely. There would have to be a factor intimately related to them in some way. If I could only attract her attention! No matter what I say, she just lies there and gurgles." He went back to his urgent buzzing, frantically using a lifetime of archaeological knowledge.

Donelli looked at the fuel indicators. His lips flattened into a grimace.

"I'll have to go out there and pick up those Q particles in the cave. That cage you built may make that avian comfortable, but it sure drained us dry."

"Wait, I'll go with you," Helena suggested. "Maybe I can discover what makes these fearsome caves so fearsome."

She donned a space suit. Donelli, after a rueful glance at his corroded helmet, dragged another metallic garment out of the locker and used its headpiece instead. They both inspected their supersonics carefully. He approved her casual efficiency.

"You know," her voice said into his headphones as they trudged toward the hill, "if Dr. Blaine is able to talk some sense into that creature and we manage to jet to a regular traffic lane and get rescued, he'll make quite a smash before the Galactic Archaeological Society with his two coexisting but unrelated civilizations. I'll get some fair notice myself with the little I've been able to deduce about these creatures biologically without resorting to dissection. Even Ibn Yussuf, bed-ridden as he is, has been doing some heavy thinking on the chemistry of a bromide soil. And you—well, I imagine you want to get back to a place where you can hurry up and get drunk."

"No."

Her helmet turned toward him in surprise and question.

"No," he continued. "If we get out of this, I'm going to take advantage of the lifeboat law. Heard of it?"

She hadn't. Her eyes glowed intently behind her visor.

"The lifeboat law's one of the oldest in space. Any spaceman—Able or Ordinary—who, under a given set of circumstances, is entitled to assume command of a vessel and successfully brings that vessel to safety may, at his written request, be issued the license of a third officer. It's called the lifeboat law because that's what it usually pertains to. I have the experience. All I need is the ticket."

"Oh. And what would you do as a third officer? Get drunk whenever you left Io?"

"No, I wouldn't. It's hard to explain—maybe you can't understand—but as a third mate, I wouldn't get drunk. An A.B. or an ordinary spaceman, now, there's so much tiresome, unimportant work facing you whenever you leave a port that you just have to get drunk. And the longer you've been in space, the drunker you get. As a third mate, I wouldn't drink at all—except maybe on vacations. As a third mate, I'd be the dryest, stiffest guy who ever was poisoned by a second cook. I'd be a terror of a third mate, because that's the way things are."

"Look at that!" Helena had paused with her back to the mouth of the cave.

Primitive War

Jake Donelli turned and looked back at the ship. Across it, in the grove of fleshy purple flowers, were at least a dozen winged creatures like the one Blaine was attempting to interest in conversation. Far over the sea, were many dots that grew larger and resolved into even more of the avians. Some of them towed gliders lightly behind them. Others carried light tubes. Blowguns?

"Wonder how they knew about Susie," the spaceman mused. "Was it because she didn't come back at the usual time that the posse was organized? Or are they telepathic?"

"A combination, possibly. They certainly seem to know when one of them is in trouble. You wouldn't say they're acting belligerent?"

"Nope. Just flexing what passes for their muscles. They don't know whether we intend to serve Susie fricasseed or boiled in her *hic jacet*. Better duck inside."

The biologist became her crisp self the moment she saw the white worms. "Wish I could tell exactly what it is they're eating. Now suppose I make a loose guess. Yes, it could well be. Jake, where are those other eggs?"

"Other eggs? Back there. Funny kind of eggs."

She slipped ahead of him, her searchlight picking out the chest-high globules. With a muttered exclamation, she bent down and examined one closely. It was slowly splitting along a pink vein. Donelli waited hopefully.

"No." She straightened. "It doesn't add up. Even assuming, as would seem possible, that those small creatures in the front are the live young of the burrowers and these are the eggs of the avians, it still doesn't explain their relative distance from the usual habitat of their parents. If they *were* the young of each species, the positions should be reversed. With their strong taboos and respective phobias, the avians would not fly so far into the cave, and the burrowers would not crawl so close to the surface. Furthermore, they would inevitably have passed each other at some time and know of each other's existence. Then too, while birth taboos are common among all primitive races, they hardly have the force of the psychoses which seem to affect both species relative to this and other caves. I'd need a good deal of study and many, many careful notes to work this problem out."

"Continu-um!" he swore. "This isn't a research paper for some scientific society or other. We're in a hurry. This is a matter of life and death, woman! Can't you put some pressure into your thinking?"

She threw up her arms in their ungainly wrappings helplessly. "I'm sorry, Jake. I'm trying hard, but I just don't have enough facts on which to base an analysis of two separate unfamiliar societies. I'm not a sociologist; I'm a biologist. So far as these creatures are concerned, I've just reached the threshold."

"That's all we do—stand around on the threshold," Donelli muttered. "Here are these caves, the threshold to our survival if we can get these babies to pick up the Q and bring it to us. The avians fly around the threshold in the underground but won't go in, while the burrowers crawl around the threshold to the surface but won't go further if you gave them the place."

"And both races are on the threshold to civilization. I wonder how long they have been there?"

The spaceman slung the inerted lead container to the ground, preparatory to catching up the crystals of contra-Uranium.

"What's the matter with them anyway that they're so afraid of the caves? What do they think will happen to them after they cross the threshold?"

"What—do—they—think—will—happen," Helena repeated slowly. "What are we all afraid of, the fear intrinsic to any living animal? But how—the eggs—why, of course! *Of course!*"

She bent toward him briefly and Donelli felt his helmet *clang*.

"Sorry," she said. "I forgot. I tried to kiss you. What beautiful reasoning, Jake!"

"Huh?" He felt absurdly clumsy in his ignorance—and guilty.

"I'll have to work the details out as I go. Dr. Blaine—once I give him your premise—he'll be able to help. Isn't it wonderful how removal of one stone from the pyramid of obscurity sends the whole structure tumbling down? Now, Jake, do you think you could go into those tunnels and fetch me a live but slightly stunned burrower? We'll need one, you know."

"I—I guess I can. Where do you want him?"

"It, Jake, it! Bring it right here to the middle of the cave. I'll be waiting for you. Hurry!"

*

She ran out of the cave toward the ship. Donelli watched her go, decided he couldn't recall any particularly clever remarks he had made, set his supersonic for its lowest frequency and moved to the tunnels.

He paused before the intersection. He and Blaine had had their little scrap with the burrowers in the right-hand one, and an elaborate trap might have been set there against their return: accordingly he chose to walk down the shaft on his left.

It was much like the other shaft. Carefully carved cross-beams were set up at intervals, while the sides were smooth and round. He came to the sharp slope and moved more cautiously. If he slipped into a hole, there was no telling how far he might fall.

The slope became steeper. Donelli's helmet light suddenly exposed another, more complicated intersection ahead in the form of six tunnel entrances. In front of one, two burrowers were chipping the end of a large root out of the tunnel ceiling.

As his search beam hit them, they whirled simultaneously and waved the hairy appendage at him for the barest fraction of a second. Then, both sprang for the tunnel entrance in a flicker of ivory bodies.

Donelli thought he had missed. He had brought up his weapon just as they leaped. But one fell to the floor, the ax-head dropping. The creature was not completely unconscious, gobbling weakly at him as he approached. Donelli slung it over his shoulder and started back. The creature squirmed limply in his grasp.

There was an odd, insistent patter behind him, a sound of many legs.

Pursuit. Well, they wouldn't dare follow him into the cave. He wished the suit weren't so heavy, though. He kept turning his head to look at the empty shaft to the rear. Nasty to be overcome from behind, under the suffocating earth of an alien planet.

Even though the burrower stiffened with fear when he reached the cave, he felt better. The pattering grew louder, stopped, came on slowly.

Helena Naxos and Blaine were squatting near the four large veined balls, the avian, weakly fluttering, between them. They held a supersonic over it. The winged creature had evidently had a dose of sound like that of Donelli's captive. Blaine was speaking persuasively, in that hum-drone language, with little apparent effect.

"Put it right down here, next to the other one," Helena ordered. "With a little time and a little imagination, we may get out of this fix. Too early to tell just yet. Jake, you'll have to act as sort of armed guard at this conference. We mustn't be disturbed. Susie's playmates are too frightened to come in, but they've been making all kinds of fuss since we carried her out of the ship and into the cave."

"I'll take care of it," the spaceman promised.

He gasped with sheer astonishment when he reached the entrance of the cave. The saffron sky was obscured by multitudes of black winged avians dipping in short angry circles. A swarm of the avians had surrounded the lifeboat and, as he watched, they lifted it slightly off the ground in the direction of the sea. This was no attempt to placate a deity, he decided, but sheer vindictiveness—revenge for the unspeakable tortures they imagined the humans were venting on the prisoner.

The supersonic low-power beam rolled them off the ship in a huge stunned mass. Their places were immediately taken by others. Donelli sprayed them off too.

They left the ship alone after that, and came in flying low at him with their blow tubes in their mouths. Jagged darts shrilled nastily all around him. He felt one bounce off his chest and hoped vaguely that they were less effective than the weapons of the burrowers on Grojen shielding. He moved back into the shadow of the cave.

Helena, Dr. Blaine and the two aliens came up behind him and gathered round the white worms near the entrance.

"Pretty dangerous here," he told them. "These avians of yours are an accurate bunch of snipers."

"No help for it," she replied. "We're getting close. I don't think they'll keep blowing darts after they get a glimpse of Sister Susie. We'll be safe so long as we're near her. Suppose you do something about the other side. Those burrowers are throwing an awful lot of stuff awfully far."

*

He moved past them toward the rear, noting that both the winged and clawed creature were no longer under the influence of the supersonics but were listening intently to Dr. Blaine as he alternately hummed at one and clicked at the other. They almost watched Helena gesture to the white worms and their grisly meal and back to them.

At least we've got their interest, Donelli thought grimly.

He began to cough. No mistake this time, there was HF vapor seeping into his suit through some scratch. Fluorine was eating at his lungs. Well, he didn't have time to feel sick.

The ivory-colored animals had rigged up a primitive ballista just a few feet from the end of the tunnel and were pegging ax-heads into the cave at fairly respectable velocities. The missiles were easy to side-step; but Donelli's head was getting heavy and he lost his footing once or twice. As fast as his supersonic would sweep them away from the ballista, they would crowd back again with stubborn determination. A slow, evil fire built itself in Donelli's chest and spread nibbling fingers along his throat.

He looked over his shoulder. No more darts were coming in at the rapt group near the cave mouth. Evidently the avians were possessed of more love for one of their number than the burrowers. He had just started to turn his head, when a heavy object struck the back of his helmet. He dimly perceived he was falling. It seemed to him that the burrower which he had captured leaped over him and rejoined its fellows, and that Susie flew out to a clustered bunch of avians and that they all buzzed and hummed like idiots.

What a waste of time, he thought as the fire began to consume his brain. Helena let them go.

It seemed to him that Helena and Dr. Blaine were hurrying to his side through a shimmering mist of yellow agony. It also seemed to him that one of the chest-high balls split up along a pink vein and something came out.

But he was sure of nothing, but the painful, choking darkness into which his body twisted, nothing but the agony in his chest . . . .

He woke with a spaceman's certain knowledge of riding a smooth jet. His body felt deliciously light. He tried to sit up, but he was too weak to do more than turn his head. Two men had their backs to him. After a while he identified them as Dr. Archibald Blaine and Dr. Douglas Ibn Yussuf. Dr. Yussuf was out of his cast and was arguing in an animated fashion with Blaine over a white ax-head imprisoned in a plastic block.

"Why, I'm in Dr. Yussuf's bunk," Donelli muttered stupidly.

"Welcome back," Helena told him, moving into range of his watery eyes. "You've been pretty far away for a long, long time."

"Away?"

"You ate enough hydrofluoric acid to etch a glass factory out of existence. I made my biological education turn handsprings to save that belligerent life of yours. We used up almost every drug on the ship and Dr. Yussuf's organic deconverter-and-respirator, which he built and used on you, is going to make him the first physical chemist to win a Solarian Prize in medicine."

"When—when did we take off?"

"Days ago. We should be near a traffic lane now, not to mention the galactic patrol. Our tanks are stuffed with contra-Uranium, our second jet is operating in a clumsy sort of way and our converter is functioning as cheerily as any atomic converter ever did. After the help we gave them with their own lives, the population of Maximilian II was so busy bringing us Q that we ran out of inerted lead containers. From considering us the personifications of death, they've come to the point where they believe humans go around destroying death, or at least its fear. And it's Jake Donelli who did that."

"I did, did I?" Donelli was being very cautious.

"Didn't you? That business about the threshold of life and death being the caves was what I heard you develop with my own ears. It was the only clue I needed. The caves related not only to the sacredness of birth, but—more important to the primitive mind—to the awful terror of death. A threshold, you called it. And so it was, not only between life and death, but between the burrowers and the avians. Once I had that, and with a little scientific guessing, it was simple to figure out why the eggs were laid in apparent reverse order—that of the burrowers near the front, and that of the avians at the rear—and why they had never met each other."

*

The spaceman thought that over and then nodded slowly.

"Simple," Donelli murmured. "Yes, that might be the word. This little shred of scientific guessing you did, just what did it amount to?"

"Why, that the avians and the burrowers were different forms of the same creature in different stages of the life-process. The winged creatures mate just as their powers start to decline. Before the young hatch, the parents seek out a cave and die there. The young, those white worms, use the parental bodies as food until they have grown claws and can travel down to the tunnels where they become adolescent burrowers.

"The burrowers, after all, are nothing but larva—despite the timbering of their shafts and their mining techniques which Drs. Blaine and Yussuf consider spectacular. They can be considered sexless. After several years, the burrower will return to the cave. In the belief of its fellows it dies there, since it returns no more. It spins a cocoon—that's what those large green balls were—and remains a chrysalis until the winged form is fully developed. It then flies out of the cave and into the open air where it is accepted by the so-called avians as their junior. It evidently retains no memory of its pre-chrysalis existence.

"Thus you have two civilizations unaware of each other, each different and each proceeding from the same organism. So far as the organism was concerned in either stage, it went to the cave only to die, and, from the cave, in some mysterious fashion, its own kind came forth. Therefore, a taboo is built up on both sides of the threshold, a taboo of the most thoroughgoing and binding nature, the mere thought of whose violation results in psychosis. The taboo, of course, has held their development in check for centuries. Interesting?"

"Yeah!"

"The clue was what was important, Jake. Once I had it, I could relate their life-cycle to the *Goma* of Venus, the *Lepidoptera* of Earth, the *Sislinsinsi* of Altair VI. And the clincher was that one of the winged forms hatched out of a cocoon just after I'd finished explaining what was up to that moment only my hypothesis."

"How did they take it?"

"Startled at first. But it explained something they were very curious about and swept away an immense weight of ugly fear. Of course, they still die in the caves to all intents and purposes. But they can see their lives as a perfect reproductive circle with the caves as a locus. And what a reciprocity they can work out—they are working out!"

"Reciprocity?" Donelli had almost moved to a sitting position.

Helena wiped his face with a soft cloth. "Don't you see? The burrowers were injuring the avian gardens by nibbling at the roots. They will now use only the roots of old, strong plants which the surface creatures will designate and set aside for them. They will also aid avian horticulture by making certain the roots have plenty of nourishing space in which to grow. In return, the avians will bring them surface plants which are not available to tunnel creatures, while the burrowers provide the surface with the products of their mines and labors underground. To say nothing of the intelligent rearing they can now give their young, though at a distance. And when the fluorescent light system that Dr. Ibn Yussuf worked out for them becomes universal, the avians may travel freely in the tunnels and guide the burrowers on the surface. The instinctual and haphazard may shortly be supplanted by a rich science."

"No wonder they broke their backs getting Q. And after working that out

31

for them, all you did was repair the ship, fix me up, take off and set a course for the nearest traffic lane?"

She shrugged her shoulders. "Dr. Blaine helped quite a bit with the take-off. This time he remembered the buttons! By the way, as far as the record is concerned, he and I maneuvered the ship off the ground under your direct supervision."

"Oh, so?"

"Just so. Right, Dr. Blaine?"

The archaeologist looked up impatiently. "Of course. Of course! There has not been one moment, since the disaster aboard the *Ionian Pinafore*, when I have not been under Mr. Donelli's orders."

There was a pause in which Dr. Blaine muttered to Dr. Yussuf over the ax-head.

"How old are you, Helena?" Donelli asked.

"Oh—old enough."

"But too clever, eh? Too educated for me?"

She cocked her head and smiled at him out of a secret corner of her face. "Maybe. We'll see what happens after we get back to the regular traffic lanes. After we're rescued. After you get your third mate's ticket. Here—what are you laughing at?"

He rumbled the amusement out of his throat. "Oh, I was just thinking how we earned our Q. By teaching a bunch of caterpillars that butterflies bring babies!"

www.ingramcontent.com/pod-product-compliance
Lightning Source LLC
Chambersburg PA
CBHW050910120626
46554CB00003B/1108